For four very special French girls...
Brune, Stella, Leonie, and Jeanne.   D.H.

For Peter van Noord and Johan van Zyl –
for their love of Paris and of cats.   P.G.

For teacher resources and more information,
visit www.tinyowl.co.uk
#ParisCat

Copyright © Tiny Owl Publishing 2020
Text © Dianne Hofmeyr 2020
Illustrations © Piet Grobler 2020

Dianne Hofmeyr has asserted her right under the Copyright, Designs and
Patents Act 1988 to be identified as Author of this work.

Piet Grobler has asserted his right under the Copyright, Designs and Patents Act 1988
to be identified as Illustrator of this work.

First published in the UK in 2020 and in the US in 2020 by Tiny Owl Publishing, London.

A catalogue record for this book is available from the British Library.
A CIP record for this book is available from the Library of Congress.

UK ISBN 978-1-910328-59-0
US ISBN 978-1-910328-62-0

PARIS CAT

DIANNE HOFMEYR
PIET GROBLER

TINY OWL

Cat was born in Paris — not on a grand boulevard but in a narrow, smelly alleyway behind the fishmonger's stall.

She grew up with hordes of brothers, sisters, cousins, aunts, uncles, and friends all squabbling over the tastiest pickings — fish heads, fish tails, fish eyes, cockle shells to lick, and a crab or two to pick.

But Cat wanted to see more of the world.
One night to escape the rain, she slunk
into a crowded café where a lady was singing.

"Pffh!"
Cat blew air from the side
of her mouth as French cats do.
"I can do that!" she mewled.
"Everyone knows cats can sing."
But it didn't end well.

"Stop that caterwauling!"

"You don't belong here!"

"Scat, alleycat!"

Out in the rain, Cat climbed a fire escape and slipped through an opening into a dark room. Under a huge table she found a nest of silk and satin, tulle and taffeta, velvet and voile and fell fast asleep.

When she woke, it was to the *scrimp scrimp* of scissors and the *whirr whirr* of sewing machines. On every side hung rails of the most exquisite dresses.

She narrowed her eyes and watched carefully. Being a French cat, she understood every instruction Madame Delphine was giving her seamstresses in the atelier.

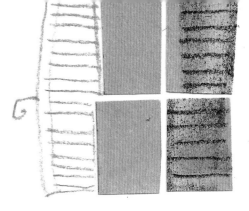

"A little tuck here."

"A pleat there."

"The fabric must cascade!"

"Pffh!" Cat blew air from the side of her mouth. "I can do that! Everyone knows cats' claws are good at pulling threads."

So that evening when the door of the atelier clicked shut, Cat gathered up the finest snippets and jumped on to the cutting table.

The scissors were large and heavy but *scrimp scrimp* she managed.

Then she claw-stitched the pieces bit by bit and sewed on a few spangly sequins.

Voilà! She was dressed to the nines.

Down the fire escape she slid, then
sauntered in her best catwalk style
into a nightclub where a lady was
dancing alongside a cheetah
wearing a diamond collar.

JOSEPHINE BAKER

"Pffh! I can do that.
Everyone knows cats are good dancers."

So she jumped on to the stage and joined the chorus line.
And WOW was she nimble on her tiny cat feet!

Now when Chiquita saw Cat, she put out her paw,
"Come dance with me, Kitty!" she purred.

And so Cat did!

She swung her satiny hips to the swinging,
jazzy beats and the audience clapped and cheered for more.

"Promise to come back tomorrow, Kitty," Chiquita purred.

And so Cat did! And every night she arrived in a new outfit made with snippets from Madame Delphine's atelier. Then she danced the night away.

Soon she was famous –
so famous that her name appeared
next to Josephine Baker's and Chiquita's
on every poster.

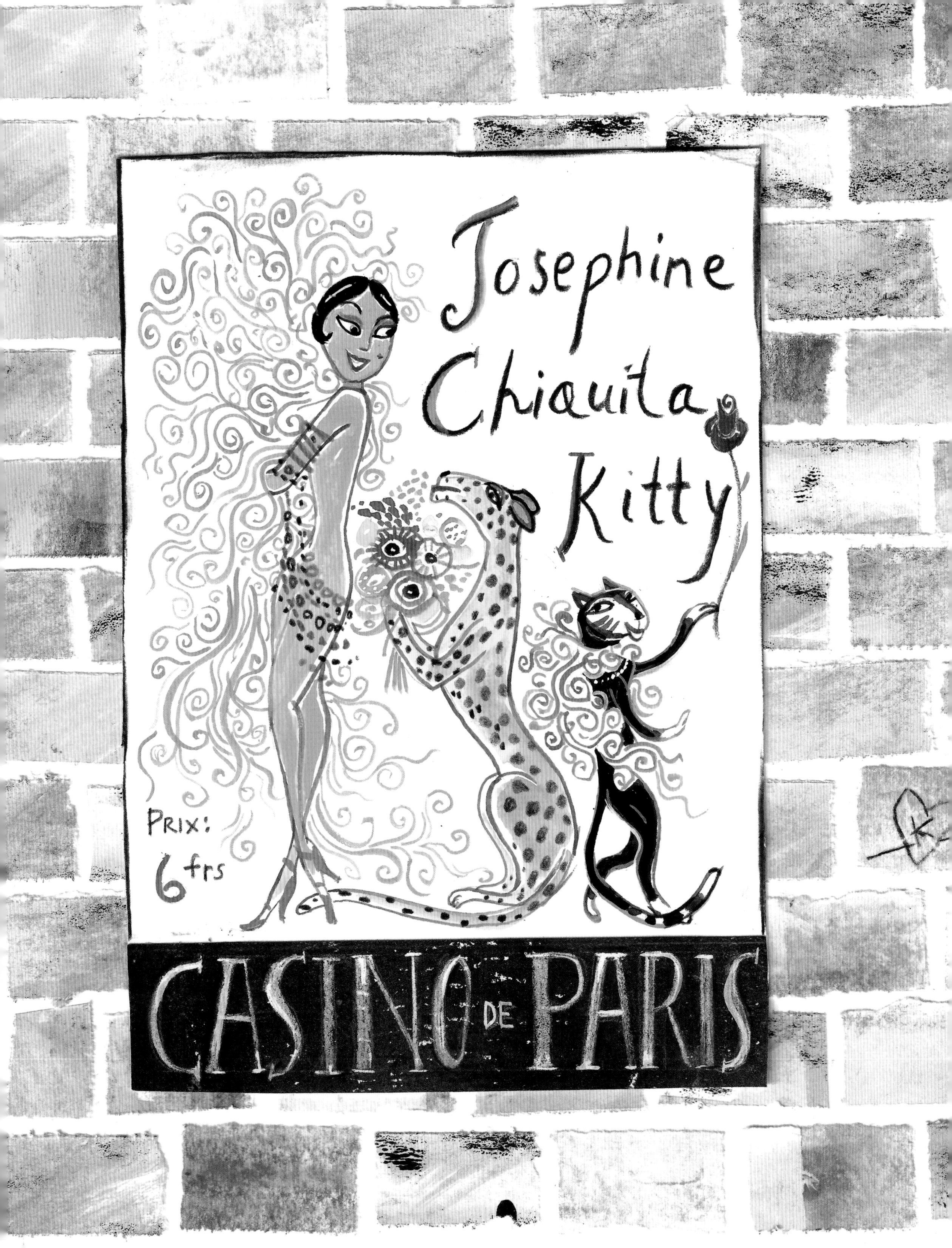
Josephine
Chiquita
Kitty
PRIX:
6 frs
CASINO DE PARIS

But Cat grew restless.

She missed all her family and friends from the old alleyway, despite all their squabbling.

So Madame Kitty's
Catacombs Club
opened in Paris.

Now if you hear loud music coming from
a cellar down a dark alleyway behind a
fishmonger's stall, and you peer in, don't be
surprised to see cats dancing the night away
in the most amazing outfits – all made by
the very sharp claws of Madame Kitty.

If you're lucky, you might even catch
a glimpse of Madame Kitty herself. But if
you don't, perhaps it's because she's off
exploring and making a new life.
Cats have nine lives, after all...

But one thing you can be sure of — to this day,
everyone at Madame Delphine's atelier is puzzled
by the fact that no snippets of cloth are ever
found under the cutting table.

THE AMAZING LIVES OF ÉDITH PIAF AND JOSEPHINE BAKER

Édith Piaf was born in Paris in 1915. She had a tough childhood and was brought up by her grandmother. At age seven she traveled in a circus caravan with her acrobat father through Belgium and France and ended up singing on the streets of Paris.

Her talent was spotted by a man who gave her a chance to sing in his nightclub. She was so tiny, he named her *la môme piaf* – the little sparrow. She was famous for the passion she put into her singing.

During the Second World War, Édith worked for the French Resistance helping prisoners of war escape. She continued to sing in Paris and even performed for Princess Elizabeth and Prince Philip in Paris in 1948.

Josephine Baker was born in the United States in 1906 to a poor family. Like Édith, she also had a tough childhood and sang on street corners.

Josephine worked her way to New York and joined a dance troupe and traveled to Paris with them. She was famous for her dancing but she never forgot her own difficult childhood and adopted 12 children from different countries and religions.

During World War II, Josephine worked for the French Resistance too and made secret notes in invisible ink on music sheets and gave them to the Allies. She was given the Chevalier of the Legion of Honor for her work. In the United States, she was a passionate activist for Civil Rights and made a speech alongside Martin Luther King in 1963.